ARE THE DAFFODILS UP

TOM HENEGHAN

Printing: Heneghan Printers.
                         135a Richmond Road
                         Fairview
                         Dublin 3
                         D03 CR64

ISBN: 978-0-9539613-13

Published (2008) By: Tom Heneghan

                        Phone: 087- 7737729
                        Email: tomhany@yahoo.co.uk

CONTENTS

THE BIG SNOW

A neighbour got sick in Ballyshaun, and my uncle
Martin went for the Priest.
It was a four mile journey to Castlebar, and there
were few cars in those days.
Even the few that existed were off the road for a
time in that particular year of 1947.
It was the year of the big snow, so most places
were no go.
A helicopter would have been the best mode of
transport, if you had a helicopter.
Anyway Martin set off on foot for Castlebar,
slipping and sliding along the way.
It took him four hours to reach the presbytery; a
mile an hour.
After being greeted by the Priests he rested and
had a warm up.
Fr William Walsh was chosen to make the journey
to Ballyshaun.
He left for his destination at 7 o'clock on this white
winter evening.
His mode of transport was also to slip and slide, but
he got there.
He got a great welcome from the Ballyshaun family,
and then anointed the sick Lady.
After a rest and a warm up he set out on the return
journey to Castlebar.

At two o'clock in the morning he trudged through the town covered in snow.

'Look at Santa Clause', shouted the men leaving the pubs.

He chuckled to himself because he knew them, but they did not recognise him.

He often chatted with those men later, but never revealed who Santa Clause was.

It's an extraordinary story, but maybe quite common in those days.

'The story of those times must be written', said Fr William to me many years later.

Now this one is written anyway.

There are a millennium of changes since, but material wealth brings its own problems.

What persecution and hunger failed to accomplish materialism has done easily.

That is the loosening of the grip the people have had on the Faith.

One of the paradoxes of life!

However, heroic deeds are still done today in a changed world.

Incidentally, the big snow of 1947 lasted for four long months.

My uncle Martin died later that year at the young age of 27.

Fr William Walsh has just passed away, as I write, at the great age of 97.

LIFE IS A MYSTERY

Life is a mystery so they say
but I knew it anyway
Look at a raindrop on a window-pane
or a snowflake that will not remain
An old shoe by the side of the road
maybe worn by a man with a heavy load
The daffodil buried in the winter earth
in the springtime comes to birth
It's amazing what life can bring
sometimes it makes us sing
World changes in the last century
makes us think a-plenty
Man went to the moon some time ago
what he saw will we ever know?
Down on earth there is a lot to ponder
will we figure it out I wonder
So far our thoughts can go
then we say I don't know
It all depends on God you see
that's why life is a mystery

MY OWN MEMORIES

BROWNES OF BREAFFY

I wandered in to Breaffy House Hotel and you would imagine Gay Nevin was waiting for me.
I asked if anybody had made out a little history of Brownes of Breaffy.
He told me he had, he gave it to me, and I was gone in five minutes.
I was amazed to get it so handy, but I have only space for a tiny bit here.
My Grandfather Michael worked in Brownes for 42 years and uncle Pat for 21.
They lived just above the wood, across the railway, in Ballyshaun.
The first Browne to arrive in Breaffy, towards the end of the 17th century, was John.
He was granted 200 acres of land in the townlands of Ballyshane and Barney.
The estate was expanded in the 18th century when his grandson, Dominick, built a house.
At their peak the Brownes added another house at the end of the 19th century.
The architecture of this house, Breaghwy Lodge, being in the Victorian style.
In 1928 most of the villages of the Browne estate were sold to the tenants.
The house and 400 acres were sold to the Land Commission.

Una and Michael Lee bought the house and 40 acres in the year 1962.

Breaffy House became Breaffy House Hotel in 1963 when a grade A hotel was opened

In 1984 the Hotel was bought by the Jennings group and goes from strength to strength.

Today Breaffy House, its grounds and woodlands, survive as a showpiece of Breaffy.

The gates are open for visitors to enjoy the wildlife, flowers and trees.

At the front of the house stands a 200 year old black Mulberry Tree.

The last of the Brownes was Dominick Andrew Sidney who left in 1961.

He was President and one of the chief organisers of the famous Breaffy Sports

He died in 1982 and is buried in the Church of Ireland Cemetery, Castlebar.

Another way of life had passed away, but Breaffy House goes on.

The old merging into the new, the past into the present and future.

If the old mulberry tree could speak or write it would have a fascinating story to tell.

But its silence, apart from the russle of leaves in the breeze, is also golden.

Let's bloom where we are planted in whatever year we are planted.

THE WOOD

One fine autumn day,
Far from the month of May
To Breaffy House I wander
What's in here I wonder

   I drive down the avenue
   Wondreous trees are not few
   The leaves all turning brown
   An odd one falling down

Then I see the old castle
The structure causes me baffle
Great builders we had in the past
Those structures they last and they last

   Down through the woods I go
   Tranquility makes me go slow
   The trees incredibly still
   Return here I surely will

Hawthorn blossom and woodbine
Around the briar entwine
I'm lucky I found this place
An oasis of gentle space

The sound of the stream relaxes
It's better than thinking of taxes
A little squirrel I see
He pretends not to see me

In a world so full of pain
My sanity here I regain
Far from the maddening crowd
Here peace is shouting out loud

THE KITCHEN TABLE

Totsie Walsh said I should call my next book (this
one) 'The Kitchen Table'.
So the least I can do is to have one chapter of that
very title.
She said the kitchen table was used for so many
important things.
Even the Eucharist occasionally.
That reminded me of the Stations I used to serve as
an altar boy.
Every year a different household in the Parish held
the stations.
The origin of the word 'Stations' escapes me now,
but in this case it is the Mass.
Anyway when a house was picked the preparations
went on for months.
No stone left unturned to have everything spick,
spotless and span.
The big day arrives and there is a roaring fire in the
big open hearth fireplace.
Shining cups, saucers and plates decorate the newly
painted open dresser.
The kitchen table covered with a white cloth is
transformed into an Altar.
The house is now a Chapel, and the neighbours
a small congregation.

The woman of the house gives an odd glance
through the small window.

'Shee, shee', she says, 'the Priest is here' as she runs
to the door to greet him.

'God Bless all here', says the Priest. 'The same to
you Father', all reply.

As he dresses for Mass a few humurous remarks
relaxes the atmosphere.

At the Consecration everybody goes still, as the
crackling fire blazes.

After Mass there is a collection and one by one the
congregation disappears.

The Chapel becomes a house once more, and the
Altar becomes a table.

Back in the room there is another table prepared
for breakfast.

The man of the house gets a special place beside
the Priest; whether he likes it or not.

Finally the Priest bids farewell and the family
can begin to relax.

The kitchen table is now restored to it's normal
everyday function.

For many a long year the old table held a variety of
material food.

On this special day it was given the honour of
holding the Spiritual.

In the quiet of the evening the family reminesce
around their faithful kitchen table.

THE CHAPEL ON THE HILL

The evening Sun shines through the stained glass
Forming its colours upon the dark brown oak.
Flowers stand in a vase in the shaded area
The altar candles give a slight flicker

A semi-nostalgic feeling creeps over my being
Blending in with the semi-empty pews
An odd cough echoes through the rafters
Whispering Ladies and the chirp of a bird

A faint distant sound gathers momentum
The train thunders by shaking the structure
Two different worlds clash in an instant
The hustle and bustle and the stillness within

Hurtling on the journey to its next destination
The trains faint whistle now part of our mood
The sinking Sun, the darkened side aisles
The old Lady with bowed head

Drawing us deeper the organ starts to play
'Abide with me, fast falls the eventide'
We are where we are meant to be
Praying in the Chapel on the hill

MY OWN MEMORIES

JOHANNA

Sometimes as I dug in the garden Johanna might
pass on her way from school.
Up the shaded boreen on the final leg of her journey
homewards
Even though she seemed quiet she stopped once to
answer my questions
'What's your name'? 'Johanna'. 'That's a lovely
name'. She smiles.
'What class are you in'? 'First class'. How was
school today'? 'Good'.
Off with her then to share the days happenings with
her Parents'.
She had the childhood joys of experiencing all the
seasons of nature on the boreen.
Winter's frost, Spring's growth, Summer's bloom,
and Autumn's nostalgia.
Johanna passed away from those life experiences at
the tender age of seven.
Seven is too young to die some might say; is 33 too
young to die?
Some die young, others die old, and some die
somewhere in the middle.
The important thing is not so much how long we
live, but how we live.
We need to be just ourselves, natural, while we are
down here.

The years have passed and Johanna would now be an adult of about thirty.

In reality though she will always be seven, or maybe just eternal.

I sometimes take a glance at her headstone in Guesdian graveyard.

'Johanna Staunton died 8th October 1984', and she leaves us with the memories.

My memories are very few compared to her Parents, brothers and sisters.

They have all the memories, a large book of memories stored away.

I have seen her on just a few occasions as she passed quietly by to her home on the hill.

But I always remember the time she stood to calmly answer my questions.

A cherished memory!

I continue to dig the garden of time while she is gone to the garden of eternity.

She passed away from this life as the brown autumn leaves fell from the trees.

The rest of us struggle on, but Johanna's memory will help us carry on.

Spring seems so far away in the dark winter nights, but it always comes.

'Let the little children come to me, for their's is the Kingdom of Heaven'

(My niece's first poem)

MYSELF

I am an Irish Child
Friendly nice and mild
Often thinking of a pleasant thought
Oh, how I wonder how I fought

Sometimes things go wrong
But I like to sing a song
Happy most of the time
It's better than cryin'

Peering through the scenery
Like some hard machinery
Nice and bright in the morning
Rarely given a warning

Spiders give me a fright
Always sleeping tight
Well that's the end of this poem
Hope you read it at home

Sabrina Grigore
(Age 10)

MY OWN MEMORIES

NO PLACE LIKE HOME

I remember in my younger days whenever I left
Ireland I got homesick.
Even if it were only for a week I always wanted to
get back quickly.
Once inside the Island of Ireland I felt happy enough
I was home.
The World is getting smaller by the day of course so
my feelings may change.
We always take home for granted because at the end
of the day we say; 'I'm going home'.
Back to our refuge after the hustle, bustle, and
happenings of the day.
A beautiful song about home was written by a man
with no stationary home.
Sadness set in as he was always on the move with a
Drama Business.
John Payne wrote 'Home Sweet Home' with an
image of his Mother in a thatched cottage.
The U.S. President heard the song and offered this
man a home in America.
As he was nearing the coast, and his new home, he
dropped dead on the ship.
It seems sad, but the song may not have been written
if he had a stationary home.
Out of pain beauty can rise.

Our family home at Donamona has a somewhat interesting history.

The house was built around 1917 by John Matthews and his cousin John Staunton.

The Matthews family left for America in 1924.

Then the house became a Garda Barracks, Police Station, for some time.

After that a nurse moved in, so it became a Medical dispensary for another period of time.

Then Mrs Bourke came to live there, and finally the Heneghan's in 1944.

Our home was a meeting place for the grandparents of the 2006 Rose of Tralee before they wed.

They would have been Lil Tuffy of Donamona and Watt Hughes of Carnacon.

I keep in contact with one of the original occupants who lives near Boston.

She is Jane Matthews Cryan who came back to visit her old home a few years ago.

She remembers well as a child her Father building the house at Donamona.

He threw sweets over the roof and she thought they were sweets from Heaven.

We reminisce about her childhood and the sad death of her Sister Kathleen at 9 years.

She says she will return to Donamona when she is 100, so we'll look forward to that.

Home is where the heart is I suppose.

HOME TO MAYO

Away on the train I go
All the way home to Mayo
Dublin City leaving behind
Tranquillity hoping to find

Down through the plains of Kildare
Without a worry or care
Not a fence to be seen
Acres of flat fields in green

We stop at Portarlington
Under a midday sun
Passengers look for a seat
Strangers here they will meet

We're on the move again
I spot some ducks and a hen
Some sheep, a goat and a cow
Passing through Offaly now

On through the Town of Athlone
Nearly half-way home
Over the Shannon river
Tranquil in this warm weather

Now we're stopped at Roscommon
Two men chat on the platform
Others just pass through the station
Each with one's own destination

The stone walls come quickly to view
Little hills they are not few
I'm feeling a wonderful flow
I'm home in the county Mayo

BEAGAN GAEILGE

Nil ach beagan gaeilge agam' and there isn't even a
fada on the computer.
I have only a little Irish, but I am brushing up with
night classes.
Uair amhain bhi programme sa Telefis is ainm
'Trom agus Eatrom.
Liam O'Murchu spoke a mixture of Irish and
English
to stimulate interest in the native tongue.
I am writing in the same way but for a different
reason, nil a lan gaeilge agam.
Michael O'Muirchataigh loves to use some Gaeilge
during the heat of a match.
'Ta an liatroid thar an trasnan, and it's another point
for Galway.
The ball is gone into the back of the net, agus cul go
halann do Mhuigheo.
Some people think that speaking the Irish language
is a waste of time.
Nil se, because our native tongue is part of what we
are even if it's buried deep down.
Nuair a bhi me og sa scoil naisuinta I did not like, or
appreciate, the gaeilge.
However when I returned to night classes I realized I
had picked up more than I thought.
'Trasna na Dtonnta' I just discovered means: 'Across
the Waves'. Beautiful.

The Irish language came from the Celts and they originated in Central Europe.

They were an iron-age people who first came to Ireland about 500 BC.

Thanaig a lan daoine as an Domhain a fearchaint ar an Oileann glas.

I wouldn't be surprised if Martin McGuinness was teaching Irish to Ian Paisley.

It has been said that a Country without a language is a Country without a soul.

Not literally true, but the meaning is clear, forceful and strong.

Right now we seem to be heading towards an English speaking world.

To speak English is good and very useful, but to speak Irish is homely.

Nil aon tinteain mar do thinteain fein, meaning Irish in this case.

I am writing this during 'Seachtann na Gaeilge', Irish Week, close to St Patrick's Day.

In my next book I hope to have the chapter totally in Irish, le cunamh De.

To communicate is all we need, but our own native tongue gives it an extra flavour.

Ta me cinte go bhuil mistakes anseo, but remember I am only in Infants Irish class.

Saol Rundiamhrach.

THE OLD MAN

He was laid to rest beside the mill
O'erlooking the lake he knew so well
His daughter was wed just a few days before
Too weak to attend, he just lay near his door
He could hear the organ in the chapel nearby
Toning out the sound of 'here comes the bride'
His thoughts ran back to the past when he
Married Sarah Kelly in a chapel near the sea
He took her home to his house on the hill
Where a patch of ground they both did till
He had five sons and an only daughter
Most of them now live over the water
All came home for the marriage of Norah
Who took the place of his wife Sarah
For Sarah died while giving birth
To Norah who now walks this earth
While her Mother is gone to eternity
Where she unfolds the mystery
Of her life on earth till she was forty three
He passed through it all the good times and bad
The joys and sorrows, the happy days and sad
He had played his part and lived like a man
The end was near of the race he ran
The Master was waiting to call him home
So he bade farewell to the earth he had known
Now he rests in the side of the hill
O'erlooking the lake, beside the mill

MY OWN MEMORIES

SMA COLLEGE BALLINAFAD

In the late 1950's SMA meant more to our family
than the college over the road.
My baby brother was seriously ill when a new food
product came on the market.
That product was called SMA and he began to
improve once he started on it.
He hasn't looked back since.
Moving on now from the material food to the food of
the spirit if you like.
Ballinafad College was just a mile from our house,
and three from Balla.
Just 100 years ago, in 1908, the SMA Order set up in
this wooded area.
The house was originally a Blake Mansion, built in
1827, with 1,200 acres of land.
When Llewelyn Blake's wife died, no children, he
became a man of deep prayer.
Fr Zimmerman, founder of the SMA Order in
Ireland, paid a visit to Ballinafad.
After discussions Llewelyn became very interested
in the SMA mission.
In 1905 he was created a papal count by Pope Pius X
for his generousity to the missions
Not only did he donate money to the Order, but he
donated the entire Ballinafad Estate.

The SMA Order gave the Estate to the Congested Districts Board.

They then received back the house and some of the surrounding land.

A Juniorate was set up for boys who wished to join this Missionary Society.

The first class to sit their leaving certificate here in Ballinafad did so in June 1952.

As numbers increased, a magnificent classroom block and Hall were erected in 1955.

Student numbers rose to 150, with 9 SMA Priests, and a Chapel was built in 1963.

On Sundays habit-clad students tossed us sweets on their way to Lough Carra.

The SMA, Society of African Missions, was founded in France in 1836.

Bishop Melchoir Bresillac founded the Order to establish the Church in West Africa.

Ballinafad College became an open secondary school in 1967.

This day-school finished in 1975, but the Order continued on for a few more years.

The last SMA Priest to finally say goodbye to this tranquil area was Fr Michael Brady.

Information flowed to me through Fr John Horgan who spent nine years in Ballinafad.

By the way, the baby food SMA stands for: Synthetic Milk Adapted.

HOLY SATURDAY

The morning is calm, tranquil and still
Flowers stand on the window sill
In the distance the hazy Sun
Today we curb our sense of fun

He lies in a grave sleeping away
No song to sing, no word to say
How could this tragedy ever be
Our eyes are closed we cannot see

Good Friday looked bad, a black black day
When the Saviour he died far, far away
Clouds came to darken the sky
Only a few to wait and cry

Palm Sunday with strewn branches had come
Now seems so far away and gone
Time for the Saviour to suffer and bleed
Fulfilling Mankinds great, great need

In the hush of the morning we stop and wonder
Will there be lightening, rain or thunder
So far no sweet birdsong we hear
Only the crisp clear morning air

This Holy Saturday is surprisingly peaceful
A time to think and be deeply prayerful
Didn't he say later he'd rise
Beauty returning to the dark, dark skies.

Easter Sunday will be magnificently bright
At last an end to the sorrowful night
The meek Saviour has gloriously risen
Leading us on to the joys of heaven

A-CUP-A-TEA

What would we Irish be without a cup of tea?
Like a lot of things it's changing of course, and the
cappuccino has arrived.
However, the cup of tea will hardly die out, but the
art of making it has gone.
'God save all here', says the neighbour, as he enters
by the half-door.
'Sit down by the fire there Tommy, and I'll make
you a nice cupeen a tea.
'All right Mary, I can't wait long though', but he's
still there two hours later.
The kettle is already on the boil as Tommy holds his
hands towards the blaze.
'The evenings are getting short now, and do you
know there's a wintry feel in the air'.
'That's true for you', says Mary, as she takes down
the delph teapot from the dresser.
Then she warms it with some water from the singing,
boiling kettle.
She puts two spoons of loose tea in the pot from the
multi-coloured tea-tin.
She then fills it with boiling water and lets it 'draw',
covered with a tea cosy.
A far cry from the rushed tea-bag job!
'Now Tommy, that'll be ready in a few minutes and
I'll have a cup myself as well'.

'Would you like the willow pattern cup or a plain cup', says Mary.

'Arragh now don't be goin' to any trouble, all I want is a drop in me hand'.

Mary selects the willow pattern anyway and saucers to go with them.

Tommy would probably have preferred a mug, but they were not invented yet.

Maybe he had started the invention process on that very evening.

The tea had now gone through its maturing process, and was ready for pouring.

'Sit in there now Tommy and that cupeen-a-tea will warm ya'.

'Wait now until I get the willow pattern jug from the dresser for the milk'.

'You'll have me spoilt' says Tommy

'No no, when a person makes a cup of tea it should be done right'.

'True for ya Mary'.

'Now, I have a nice swiss roll cake here and I'm sure you'll have a piece'.

'Ah no, …………. well I will so'.

Mary pours a cup for herself also and settles herself up to the table.

The conversation flows freely soothed by the relaxing cup-a -tea.

THE VILLAGE I LEFT BEHIND
(BALLYKEERAN)

As I sit here in the silence
Of a room that's new to me
My thoughts wander back
To a place I used to be

Ballykeeran is the village
Just a few miles from Athlone
Memories flooding back
For years it was my home

The dog and duck down below
The shop across the bridge
The Post office up the road
St Pauls upon the hill

The Convent in the valley
The lake they call Lough Reagh
Every morning from my window
That's the view I'd see

My two friends at the gate lodge
Left the same week as me
All for different destinations
Life is a mystery

Down the road there's Glasson
The village of the roses
A model Irish village
Where the stranger reposes

31

Further on there's Tubberclair
Where the Chapel bells do ring
And the organ playing softly
While the choir wait to sing

So farewell to Ballykeeran
It's Paradise to view
To all my friends who live there
I will surely miss you

BETHLEHEM

Did you know that Ireland has a Bethlehem, and it's also a Holy Place.
It stands in the midlands beside Lough Reagh on the river Shannon.
In 1629 the Poor Clare Sisters came to Ireland to found a house in Dublin.
They were all Irish who had joined the Order some years previously in France.
Sr Marianna Cheevers from Wexford was the first to be professed there, in 1620
After a short stay in Dublin the Sisters accepted an offer of land in Westmeath.
Their new midland Convent by the lakeside they named Bethlehem.
Eventually the convent name became the place name, and so it is today.
The Parish within which Bethlehem stands is called Tubberclare; 'St Clare's Well'.
Galway-born Sr Bonaventure Browne kept precious notes about life in Bethlehem.
She was later to return to her native county and help set up a convent there.
The decision to establish that Convent was issued at Bethlehem in 1642.
The original of the document is preserved to this day in the Galway, Nuns's Island, Convent.

The Poor Clare Community at Bethlehem eventually
grew to sixty Religious.
Cecily Dillon, a local girl, was elected Abbess on
five occasions.
Her six nieces joined the Order at Bethlehem.
Adoration of the Blessed Sacrament was kept up
night and day in this tranquil area.
It was at Bethlehem that the rule, and Blessing, of St
Clare was translated into Irish.
After 11 years the Sisters took refuge on an Island in
Lough Reagh.
Their Convent was set on fire, and so there was no
return to Bethlehem.
Miraculously the tabernacle, holding the Blessed
Sacrament, was preserved.
An image of Our Lady, made from wood, was also
found in the debris.
It stands in the Galway Convent today.
After Bethlehem one group of Sisters went locally to
Athlone, and another to Wexford.
1993 was the 8th centenary of the birth of St Clare,
so Sisters converged on Bethlehem.
They came to remember with gratitude those who
lived, prayed and suffered there.
If travelling from Athlone to Ballymahon, branch
off left at Tubberclare.
It takes you on a nostalgic journey back in time to
the holy ground of Bethlehem

THE CHURCH AT TUBBERCLARE

A lonely Church stands on a hillside
In the village of Tubberclair
Where humble people come together
Bow their heads and kneel in prayer

Every Sunday at eleven you can hear the
Church bells ring
For the people to assemble and greet their
mighty King
The little choir wait in silence till the altar
boys appear
Then they raise their voice together in a
hymn of solemn prayer

In the background stands a lake peeping
through the trees
From where a mist comes moving slowly
carried by the gentle breeze
In the Church the Priest continues to pray
to God above
As he becons to the choir to sing out a
hymn of love

Round the Church there lies a graveyard to
the memory of those gone
Every headstone tells a story as we move
quietly along
But the singing from the chapel reminds us
they're not dead
Only gone to sing forever to the one who all
things made

MY OWN MEMORIES

GUESDIAN

I remember as a child listening to James Tuffy
explaining the meaning of Guesdian.
It was at a Station Mass so he had very attentive
listening ears.
Goath-as-Dun in Irish means 'wind from the castle,'
he explained.
Sure enough the old castle is there on the hill
overlooking the graveyard.
It is in an ideal position for the wind to swirl and
whistle through.
Reviving memories of a distant and different time of
centuries past.
The meander river, a tributory of the moy, flows in
the tranquil valley.
And in the wood stands the residence of the Late
Liam and Judy Coyne.
They it was who set up the Knock Shrine Society in
the year 1935.
Guesdian produced a 'Mayo Man of the Year' in the
gentle form of Fr Edward Tuffy.
The castle dates from the 13th century and I believe
the graveyard is older still.
There is the ruins of an old Church there and another
over the road in Loona.
St Patrick passed through Guesdian on his way from
Croagh Patrick to Balla, and onwards.

Pilgrims today follow in his footsteps, on Tochar
Phadraig, from Balla to the Reek.
I suppose the main feature of Guesdian today is the
graveyard beneath the castle.
There lie the rich and the poor, young and old, the
famous and not so famous.
All equal now!
Often the Priests words 'when every tear will be
wiped away' waft through the air.
Paddy Tuffy tells me that the oldest inscribed
headstone goes back to 1782.
The Castle reminds us of a different Guesdian with
lots of activity from the hill above.
It's amazing how busy places in one age become
quiet in another.
Nowadays though it seems to be one way traffic with
quiet places becoming busy.
Guesdian should remain quiet and tranquil for the
foreseeable future.
But the village of Belcarra may overflow one day,
into Guesdian, to become a town.
The most important thing about Guesdian, personally
speaking, is that my Mother was born there.
May Kilcourse rambled down the grassy boreen
before the rush of life infected us.
In the golden days of her youth.
My aunt-in-law, if there is such a term, wrote the
following poem long ago:

BELCARRA OF THE LONG LONG AGO

I am thinking tonight of a dear little spot
A place called Belcarra, cosy beneath the hilltops
With its cute little houses and neat little shops
A guards barracks where policemen did dwell
To keep peace and order they did very well

There were Tuffys the pub and Jennings also
Mick Cooney the butcher and Mrs Kilrow
Where all were welcome the high and the low
Then the school by the river where all had to go
To answer the questions we stood out in a row

Tommie Naughton the cobbler and fiddler also
To tune up his fiddle he'd first rassin the bow
Thomas McHale the weaver lived beside the big tree
With his loom and thread and its wheels running free

Pat Mullaney the tailor with his cloth cut and tacked
Maggie Heneghan who sold all kinds of nick nacks
Tom Mannion the cobbler with his hammer and
tacks
And the Post Office with its stamps, seal and wax

Pat Murray the blacksmith where all men did go
To shoe up their horses they had to stand in a row
And nestled beside him was that Chapel so grand
With its steeple and bell, the finest in the land
Calling all people in for to pray
To ask for God's Blessings on each passing day

Ah, all those people are gone now
In the graveyard they rest
May their souls shine in Heaven
The bright home of the blest

Sarah (Walsh) Heneghan

AMERICAN WAKE

Recently a Lady in Dublin decided to hold a going-
away party for her friends.
The unusual thing here being that the party was for
her departure from this life.
Her doctor had given her a short time to live, so she
had the courage to hold a party.
This was quite similar to the American wake held
in Ireland 50 to 100 years ago.
A family member for employment reasons decides to
depart for America.
The night before a party is held for family members,
neighbours and friends.
It was a true wake because in many cases they were
saying goodbye never to return.
No Jumbo Jet available to whisk them home at the
snap of the fingers in those days.
The normal wake would have a dead person in
attendance ready for burial.
Neighbours and friends usually stayed up the whole
night chatting about the deceased.
The unique joys and sorrows that this Human Being
passed through.
The interesting term used for those occasions was
'to wake the dead'.
'AH SURE' are two words I saw inscribed on a
headstone in Balbriggan recently.

Did you know that the art of embalming was invented by an Irishman.

James Scanlon from Ballymote, and America was also his work-place.

Anyway back to our American Wake, and the person is very much alive.

Just about to start out on a new adventure in a new land of opportunity.

I have not experienced any of those wakes but the pain must have been as real as death.

Death to life in Ireland to experience a new life in far off America.

Waving goodbye at Manulla Junction, and the train disappears out of sight.

Then the waiting of Parents for news, by telegram, that their 'child' had arrived safely.

The mobile phone, texts and emails seemed a million years away.

The first letter from Philadelphia which was read over again and again.

The excitement to hear that they had arrived safely, and all was going well.

Still the sad wondering 'would they ever come back to where their heart has ever been?

Some of those young people did actually return in later life, but were the Parents there?

Back to the old bog road, and memories of their American wake.

AN APRIL DAY

The dew lies soft upon a low lying field
At seven o'clock on an April morning
The cows nostrils breath out vapour
A rabbit hops by

The hazy sun peeps from the horizon
Lighting the art of the spider webs
We stare at nature in wonder
Listening to the silence

The mid-day sun covers the earth
Fluttering new leaves in the gentle breeze
Bees buzz around stopping to refuel
At a pretty bunch of primroses

A cluster of birds chirp from the treetop
In harmony with natures springtime
Winters snowdrop gives way to the daffodil
Optimism in the air.

A horse stands still behind a wooden fence
At seven o'clock on an April evening
A minnaun's song harmonises the stillness
A bat flies by

The deep red sun sinks in the west
Splashing the sky with purple stripes
Blending with the yellow furze landscape
Flooding the mind with memories

MY OWN MEMORIES

SAVING THE HAY

I saved hay for Ned and Bridgie May Kelly in
Ballydavock.
For Mark and Mrs Winters in Frenchill, and for Joe
Mitchel in Logaphuil.
I also saved some hay for Ned and Sarah O'Malley
in Kilboyne.
All this was done during school holidays, so how
much saving I did I don't know.
At a time of high unemployment there I was working
away at 11 years of age.
Nobody told me about the high unemployment, so
'what you don't know won't bother you'.
Saving the hay was somewhat like saving the turf
from a weather point of view.
You had to try and judge the weather for rain, which
wasn't easy in Ireland.
We had no monsoons, but a shower could approach
easily from the west.
If you got one dry week everything could be
completed fairly fast.
If it rained after cutting it could be a long, long
drawn-out process.
When summer arrived the scythe was taken down
and sharpened.
The sharpening stone was about one foot, half a
metre, long and fat in the middle.

Out then into the field and the swings began, soothed by the smell on new mown hay.

The sweat on the brow was constant, so a bucket of spring water stood nearby.

This was a time before modern machinery which seem to get bigger by the year.

The cut hay was left lying for a day or two and then turned with a rake.

Next it was lap-cocked, rain permitting, and then into larger cocks.

Finally it was made into a massive cock where many hands were needed.

Making the cocks was great fun because you could get lost in the hay.

Each cock was secured with a rope to stop it blowing away in the wind.

Believe it or not the rope was made from the hay itself, and that was an art worth seeing.

The sound of Sarah O'Malley's whistle in the distance called us to lunch.

I'd be the first to down tools with a glance of the eyes from Ned.

Bridgie May might arrive in her field with tea and sandwiches.

As the autumn sets in the cows stare across at the massive cock of hay.

'A job well done' says they in cow language, which is called Moo.

EIRE'S MAN OF CLAY

Ireland, Ireland
This work of art upon your land
Misty Isle look where you lay
On Europe's edge with your man of clay

Man of clay raised from the earth
On Eire's Isle you came to birth
A rugged land with stony soil
Connemara man you sweat and toil

A Celtic land in history deep
Man of clay you laugh and weep
Green, green Isle whose beauty speak
To foreign men who search and seek

Man of clay you dream to be
Of service to humanity
On foreign shore and far-off hill
Your roots are in old Eire still

MY OWN MEMORIES

WESTERN RAIL CORRIDOR

I like to stand and watch trains and planes, and
probably boats as well.
A Westport to Boston Ocean Liner service might be
a nice idea.
Maybe too slow for the modern age, but we'll keep it
as a dream anyway
For the moment let's concentrate on our homely
Western Rail Corridor.
It's not ready as I write but they are working on it,
believe me.
The corridor was originally opened, the final section
to Colloney, on the 1st October 1895.
Amazingly there's three International Airports along
the route now.
The whole line, from Limerick to Sligo, took 36
years to construct in hard times.
Not many cars about then, none actually, so its
importance was enormous.
The opposite is the case now, too many cars, so its
importance will be just as great.
From Sligo the train rolled through: Ballisodare,
Colloney, Tubbercurry, Curry.
Next into Mayo: Charlestown, Swinford, Kiltimagh,
Claremorris, Ballindine.
Through Galway: Milltown, Tuam, Ballyglunin,
Athenry, Craughwell, Ardrahan, Gort.

Then into Clare: Ennis, Six-mile-bridge, and finally on to Limerick.

During this age of tourism it will be fascinating to see that train roll again.

In 1963 diesel replaced steam, and in the same year the corridor began to break up.

The passenger service from Claremorris to Colloney stopped in 1963, and freight in 1975.

John Conroy was the last Kiltimagh Station Master; eagerly awaiting the reopening.

In 1869 Irish people have helped built the railroad across America.

One company started in the west, another in the east, until they eventually met.

Happily they met in the right place, so they joined the meeting spot with a golden spike.

The first passenger train ever ran in 1825, and the Orient Express took off in 1883.

I may be going off on the wrong track here, so back to our corridor in the west.

'West-on-Track' was set up in 2003 to campaign for the corridor's reopening

People like Fr Michael McGreal have been on the campaign trail on an ongoing basis.

Perhaps 'West-on-Track' could stay together and campaign later for a Federal Ireland.

Anyway lets hope steam is used for the first train back on this romantic line.

BLACK BEAUTY AND THE BEACH

I stood on Balbriggan beach
Humming a verse of a song
Watched a green train pass by
Carriages tagging along

I thought of times long ago
A black horse gracefully trotting
His carriage looked part of himself
Passengers happily waving

The red sun sinks in the west
Colouring the evening sky
A time to think and dream
One could live or die

A horse and carriage approaches
Is it a mirage or true
Black Beauty gracefully trotting
Passes by and loses a shoe

The train roars into the distance
As the sea in my ears resound
What would the world be like
Without our sight and sound

Turning to face the green waters
A refreshing wind meets my face
Healing here there must be
A place of beauty and grace

The beach is almost deserted
But this is one place to be
The old saying still holds true
The best things in life are free

OUR CHRISTMAS

Our first sign of Christmas was to see a little Santa
in the newspapers.
From November onwards we'd scrutinise each of
the pages meticulously.
Whoever found the first Santa was a hero, and after
that they multiplied daily.
The Christmas atmosphere had begun, with our
joyous expectations.
In a way it had started in the summer when Nan
started to fatten up young turkeys.
What a sound they made when food arrived; and
they to become food for others.
I should become a vegetarian!
Anyway we went in search of a Christmas tree and
holly with berries.
Letters to Santa had to be written, even though he
can read minds anyway.
We dreamed of a white Christmas, as Nan starts
writing her long shopping list.
Currants, raisins, cynamon and nutmeg for the
rich Christmas cake.
Unselfishly we'd help to make her long list even
longer still.
'I got a great Christmas box in Madden's this year',
said Nan after her shopping expedition.

We'd all rummage through the box to see what was
there for us.

The holidays from school were now with us, so
things were happening fast.

On Christmas Eve Santa even spoke on radio, and
read out some of our requests.

Long red candles were placed at every window
as night-time approached.

The light of the world was very near!

We listen to the weather forecast and then check
the sky for signs of snow.

'What did I tell you', said Matt as he enters with a
snowflake on his sleeve

Snugly inside we carefully hang up our stockings at
the large firside.

'Off to bed with ye now, Santa won't come until ye
are fast asleep', we were told.

Da arrives home with a poor goose for the big dinner
of next day.

Everything seems ready as we try to calm ourselves
into sleep.

The sound of 'Silent night' from the kitchen helps us
on our way.

Next morning we have the fastest rise ever to stare in
wonder at our toys.

Off to Mass then in Belcarra, and we greet the new-
Born Babe.

THE TIME IS COME
(Christmas Carol)

When time began God's link with man
Somehow, somewhere got broken
But God then knew what he would do
In the distant misty morning

Then through the years, and prophets tears
Mankind moved slowly onwards
Courage of the few carried others through
To that longed-for mystic dawning

The time is come, God sends his Son
Not in a silver cradle
In a bed of hay there Jesus lay
On a cold and frosty morning

A virgin girl he chose to be
Mother of his Son to set us free
Mary's child is born all war shall cease
That we might love and live in peace

MY OWN MEMORIES

KNOCK

Many things could be, and have been, written about
modern day Knock
The Pope's visit, The Basilica, Monsignor James
Horan, the airport on the hill.
However I'll stick to the simple story of how it
all began.
Simple but magnificent!
In Irish it's called 'Cnoc Mhuire', Marys hill,
Knock being an anglicised version.
In 1879 Knock was like a lot of Irish villages of
post famine Ireland
The small chapel being the main feature, and it's
there still.
On the 21st August Mary Mcloughlin was leaving
Mary Byrne's house.
It was pouring rain but they both noticed statues
at the gable of the Chapel
On closer inspection they discovered that they
were in fact live figures.
Mary Byrne rushed back into the house to tell her
Mother, brother and sister.
Word spread quickly and fifteen people in all saw
this amazing event.
They saw Our Lady, with St Joseph on one side
and St John on the other.

To Our Lady's left was an altar with a lamb on top,
and a large cross behind
Our Lady had her eyes raised to heaven and she
wore a beautiful white robe.
She wore a sparkling crown on her head, and a
golden rose on her forehead
Her two hands were raised to the shoulders and
facing each other.
St Joseph was slightly bent at the shoulders as
if in homage to Our Lady
St John held a book, believed to be the Gospels,
in his left hand.
A brilliant heavenly light shone on everything
at the gable.
Our Lady left no verbal message; sometimes
silence speaks louder than words.
The witnesses were aged between 5 and 75, and they
never changed their story.
They stood in awe in the pouring rain, but no rain
fell at the gable.
A trickle of pilgrims started to arrive which became
a river as time passed.
In centenary year of 1979 the Pope himself, John
Paul 11, visited Knock.
Blessing the large crowd he could see in his minds
eye the 15 humble witnesses.
'Knock and the door will open, seek and ye shall
find'.

MISTY VILLAGE

Misty village on the hill
Humble simple people
Mary came to visit here
At the Chapel gable

    Wondrous eyes watch in awe
    How could this ever be
    That the Mother of Our Lord
    Could come for us to see

Rain pours down upon the town
People standing still
Young and old out in the cold
Stood on the misty hill

    Mary Joseph and St. John
    Angels hoover round
    Altar holding Lamb and cross
    Above the holy ground

Dark clouds roll around the sky
Pierced by brilliant light
Blazing up Cnoc Mhuire Church
In the dark, dark night

    Blessed Mayo you were chosen
    To receive this vision
    What a blessing, what a joy
    To see the queen of Heaven

MY OWN MEMORIES

THE WEATHER

Sometimes you would imagine that the weather is
only here for conversation.
Of course maybe it's better to be talking about the
weather than the neighbour.
A lot of people talk about the weather without really
experiencing it.
Unless the Sun is shining we go inside, bolt the door
and suffer it until it changes.
There's actually nothing more exhilarating as to
walk through the strong wind.
If it's autumn and the leaves are blowing down it's
more wondrous still.
Wind is an amazing thing, you can't see it but it can
blow down a huge tree, and more.
Nobody likes getting wet in the rain, but it keeps our
Island green.
And if there was no rain what would we use our
umbrella's for?
A person may not stand outside for very long on a
frosty night.
However if you look up at the millions of stars it
changes everything.
One forgets about the cold and becomes starstruck
with the immensity of it all.
People may not like snow to last very long, but most
love a white Christmas.

To see a person from a far-off Land experiencing snow for the first time is fascinating.

The wonder of the white flakes falling from the sky can be awesome.

Spring brings a rise in temperature and growth is all around us.

The beauty of April 2007 may never be equalled; remember it?

Some love the hot sun of summer days with stunning evening sunsets.

I like a mild day, not too hot and not too cold, with a deep stillness.

Weather signs are there too:

Crows standing in a field means approaching rain, as does the near look of the mountains.

A red sky at night is a Shepherd's delight, and in the morning a shepherd's warning.

A Lady in England predicted a hurricane one time, it came in spite of the weatherman.

Conversation will continue about the weather, but it's more important to experience it.

As a wise woman said to me: 'won't you get out now and get plenty of fresh air'.

So the next time you see weather, cold or hot, wet or dry, just grasp it.

You probably will never see today's weather exactly the same again.

AUTUMN

Strolling in the tree covered avenue
The sound of a waterfall in the distance
Lively squirrels hopping on branches
The dark red sun sinks.

Tree leaves turn to a golden brown
A gentle breeze rustles through
The mild evening enhances the setting
Autumn is here

The feeling is good and prolonged
The present moment is all we need
No thoughts of dark winter nights
Let it come in its own time

The pram-wheeling Lady looks around
Two toddlers examine an insect
Their concentration is eager and total
The Lady smiles and moves on

A garden seat stands in a shaded area
Streams of sunlight piercing either side
There it rests under the large oak tree
Having given rest to many

The green park comes slowly to view
A chorus of children follow a football
Adult laughter hangs long in the air
The football lands at our feet

The autumn of life creeps up on us too
Hopefully mellow like the golden leaves
A time to stop, reflect, wonder and think
About Life and things.

AER LINGUS

In Ireland, or even abroad, we don't ask what
Aer Lingus means.
Straight away the image of our national airline
comes into view.
However when it comes to the meaning of the words
'Aer Lingus' we have to think.
Sounds like Latin, but I believe it's old Irish, and
they mean: 'Air Fleet'.
Aer Lingus was established in 1936, and Baldonnel
was used as the first airport
The first pilot was Captain Oliver Armstrong when
he flew 'Iolar' to Bristol.
Around this time the west of Ireland was becoming
very important in air travel.
In 1935 the Americans chose Foynes as a stopover
for their transatlantic traffic.
The planes landed on water, and Foynes became the
biggest air terminal in the world.
Aer Lingus had their first flight from the new Dublin
airport in 1940; to Liverpool.
A beautiful terminal building was erected, which is
now lost amongst the modern.
Across the water from foynes a new 'Land' airport
was set up at Rineanna.
Aer Lingus had their first transatlantic flight from
here, now Shannon, in 1958.

We sometimes heard of a neighbour heading for
far-off America.

The car journey would take them through 'The
Curragh Line' to Rineanna.

'The Curragh Line' was a seven mile stretch of road,
without a turn, outside Galway.

We longed to see that amazing road

Over the years Aer Lingus developed as flights
became longer and more numerous.

It was like a little bit of Ireland landing at different
airports around the world.

Irish people in far-off lands get a lift on seeing the
aircraft with the shamrock.

Sadly this important piece of green Ireland was
recently privatised.

I think 'Aer Lingus' is one thing that should belong
to all the Irish people.

Aircraft of different names and colour land at Dublin
now with Aer Lingus.

From a distance the airport looks like a bee-hive as
planes buzz in and out.

We have travelled a long way since the Wright
Brothers first flight

That 'long' flight took 17 seconds, and the distance
was about the length of a Jumbo.

I wonder did they forsee the great progress in flight
since; hardly

Aer Lingus: our 'Air Fleet'.

THE BUBBLE

Has anybody seen the bubble
Created by me today
If you should happen to find it
Please send it back to stay

With a grace that's rarely seen
It floated right up to the sky
How will I ever find it
More elusive than the butterfly

It is only soap and water
But it's also a beautiful queen
Formed by the master's blow
Never to be touched only seen

It's only a poor little bubble
With the flow of the wind it will go
Like a balloon only weaker
Where it will end I don't know

Then as I stand here thinking
A raindrop falls on my head
Yes, I'm sorry to tell you
The beautiful bubble is dead.

MY OWN MEMORIES

BROKEN BISCUITS

It was a time when every thing was loose; no
packaging for groceries.
If you wanted tea the shopkeeper had a large
tea chest full
A little shovel was used to fill out the required
amount into a paper bag.
The modern tea bag, round oval or square, was for a
day in the future.
When the tea chest became empty it was put to
many other uses.
The same process was used for sugar, but I think it
came in a large sack.
Flour definitely came in a large sack, and was
ordered frequently
Every housewife did her own wholesome baking,
and t'was good
Even the term 'housewife' is rare now.
Milk came in a glass bottle which seemed quite
natural at the time
A carton of milk would have been just as unusual
as a tea bag.
Imagine putting milk in a cardboard box; out of
the question.
Eggs had to be covered one by one with newspapers
to avoid breakage on the bike.

A loaf of bread went in the opposite direction, as it became loose when sliced at home.
When the sliced pan arrived it was the greatest thing since the……….
Biscuits came in a large cardboard box and were filled out into paper bags.
Sometimes Nan would come home with a box of broken biscuits.
The shopkeeper gave them out free, and it was the only way to get assorted ones.
There was great excitement when an unexpected box of broken biscuits arrived.
Each of us had our own favourite as scrambling hands searched high and low.
We had marietta, arroroot, nice, ginger nut, goldgrain
and rich tea.
Those were the plain ones, and then it was time to go for the double or fancy ones.
Kerry-creams, kimberley, coconut-cream, wafers, Mikado, figrolls.
How Jacob's got the figs into the figrolls did not concern us atall
Nan made a nice cup of tea for herself, and watched the commotion.
Gradually the supermarkets arrived and turned the shopping world upside down.
Gone is the wonderful life of the shopkeeper and the broken biscuit

BUILD THOSE BRIDGES

Build those bridges, break down the fences
In all the world in every land
Burn the story of past war and glory
Build those bridges reach out your hand

In a world where milk and honey flow
Some have nothing, others o'ergrow
In a world that's meant for you and me
Some grow hungry, in a world of plenty
Others sow seed of hatred and greed
A world where earth yields abundant wheat
Why must some have nothing to eat

In a world torn by unrest and strife
Some are asked to give of their life
In a world entrusted to humanity
Children mistreated, the weak defeated
Some wield power, thinking it's honour
A world of beauty distorted by man
Why not change it, let's start again

Build those bridges, break down the fences
In all the world in every land
Burn the story of past war and glory
Build those bridges reach out your hand

MY OWN MEMORIES

PULLING FOR LIGHTS

Outside our gateeen the road was covered with
bicycle reflectors.
Where did they all come from we wondered
out loud.
Our detective minds were put to work as we
observed the situation.
The next bicycle might give us some clue as to
what was going on.
In those days we didn't have long to wait for a
two wheeled vehicle.
Back the road comes the bicycle with its
unsuspecting occupant.
As usual our dog gave chase as part of his daily
entertainment.
We noticed that he sank his teeth into the reflector
rubber support
Out popped the reflector, unknown to the occupant,
and the mystery was solved.
How he managed such a feat on a moving vehicle
amazed us.
The dog had plenty of opportunity to practice his
unique skill.
You could say he was pulling for lights, which was
the job of the guards really.
'Pulling for lights' was one of the main occupations
of the guards, police, at that time.

If you had a bicycle out at night without a light you
got 'pulled'; meaning stopped.
I presume that the word 'pulled' came from: 'to pull
on the brakes.'
Everything has speeded up since then with tragic
consequences in some cases.
Car accidents occupy a large part of a guards
occupation nowadays.
I wonder what the alternative to the car will be in the
next century, or sooner?
Our main worry was whether there was a stone on
the road as we cycled along.
Otherwise we could almost see through the dark as
our eyes got adjusted.
Another occupation of the guards was checking that
your dog had a licence.
Our dog could be described as a guard-dog, so he
might have been exempt.
He certainly served his time pulling for lights, and
may have gone on to greater things
One man thought he should have a cheaper licence
because his dog was black and white.
Well not really, just a joke that was going around in
the good old days.
In our lit-up world of today pulling for lights rarely,
if ever, takes place.
We hope we have a more en-lightened world, but
one would have to wonder.

WONDER

To wonder about the things we see
From dawn of Life to eternity
From a planted seed to an apple tree
To wonder

I wonder about our gift of sight
To see the stars come out at night
To see the Sun shine so bright
I wonder

To wonder about the things we hear
From a blackbird song to a panting deer
From distant sounds to sounds so near
To wonder

I wonder about our gift of hearing
To hear the loud thunder peeling
Ocean waves which give that feeling
I wonder

To wonder about the things we smell
From daffodil to sweet bluebell
From open fields to planted dell
To wonder

I wonder about the smell of gas
To smell the lawn with new mown grass
The rose's fragrance as we pass
I wonder

We wonder about humanity
Trillions of fish in the Sea
The wonder of an old oak tree
Wonder-full

MINISTER IN FORTLAWN

We had a Minister for Lands, Agriculture, living
next door to us at Fortlawn.
His house nestled snugly amongst the trees, and
under the Ringfort on the hill.
Joseph Blowick was born in Belcarra, two miles
down the road, in 1903.
In moving to Fortlawn he was, in a sense, returning
to his roots.
His Mother being Nora Madden from the shop next
door, on the other side, at Donamona.
He was first elected to the Dail, Irish Government, in
the year 1943.
He became leader of 'Clann na Talmhan' (Party of
the Land) in 1944.
The party was set up in 1938 to address grievences
of small farmers in the west.
Joseph Blowick was Minister for Lands from 1948-
51 and from 1954-57.
This meant, above all else, a spin in the State-Car for
us small ones on one occasion.
He oversaw some drainage schemes amongst which
was the Moy river.
His main achievement was the encouragement of
forestry schemes.
He must have been encouraged himself by the sight
of the tree-covered Fort upon his hill.

What would this world of ours be, without the sight of a tree.

Long ago Ireland was covered with forests, so we should be leaning that way again.

Anytime I see a forest in the countryside today Joe Blowick comes to mind.

The house at Fortlawn was built around 1748 by whom I do not know.

The Mulrooney Family moved in at some stage and lived there up until 1943.

Mrs Mulrooney was well known for her ailment cures as a herbalist.

Joe Blowick took his sister Nora and brother Pat with him to Fortlawn.

He also got married to Theresa whilst residing at this secluded spot.

I sometimes mowed the lawn in front of his house under the direction of Nora.

His brother, Fr John, co-founded the Maynooth Mission to China.

This Religious Order today would be better known as the Columban Society.

Joseph Blowick moved back to Belcarra in 1961, and he passed away in 1970.

The present owners, Padraic and Bernie McGreal, moved into Fortlawn in 1962.

The Ringfort trees stand tall upon the hill as a wonderful landmark of Fortlawn.

RADIO EIREANN

My Mother's voice wakes me from slumber
O'Donnell Abu wafting from the kitchen
What day is it I wonder
Bridie Gallagher lets me know
On the old Radio

     I know I'll have Sports Stadium today
     Who will be the winner at the Curragh
     Philip Green showing Rovers the way
     The Kennedy's of Castleross, or is it
     Harbour Hotel
     Surely the story line will tell

Yesterday we took the floor
To Dinjo's voice we all did dance
One step, two step, three step, four
Tom Foley could not lead the way
Alice had the final say

     Question time with Joe Linnane
     Who wants to be a ten-pound-aire
     Who will play this wonderful game
     Bart Bastible or Morgan O'Sullivan
     Maybe Treasa Davidson

Tomorrow we will have Michael O'Hehir
Christy Ring bends, lifts, strikes
The ball is gone over the bar
One Michael passes the torch to another
To tell the flight of the sliother

Walton's last word from Leo McGuire
If you feel like singing do sing an Irish song
Which song does one require
Dublin can be Heaven, with Coffee at eleven
Good night from Radio Eireann.

THE TURF FIRE

'Come up to the fire', says Da, 'ye'll catch yer death
down there'.
He always loved to have a roaring fire in the grate of
the hearth.
Everybody round in a semi-circle staring at, and
soothed by, the blaze.
It stimulated conversation of its own kind; like the
camp fire at night.
Story-telling, jokes, memories, silences and even a
verse of a lonesome song.
In modern times there may also be a semi-circle, but
to stare at the box.
The T.V may stimulate some conversation, but
mostly it's 'keep quite'.
The turf fire is, or was, unique to Ireland.
In fact people of other countries are amazed to see
we can actually burn 'earth'.
They love to hear about the whole process of getting
this 'earth' ready for fire.
We had slaved away during the summer months
'saving the turf'.
And now we were reaping the rewards on a cold
frosty night.
The turf fire radiated the heat long before radiators
were heard of.

The fire had a bigger role to play in everyday life
than heating us of course.

Over the blaze stood the crane with hooks for pots
and singing kettle.

Always ready to make a cupeen of tea for house-hold
and stranger.

All cooking and baking took place over the blaze of
the turf fire.

The tongs stood by in a corner ready to stir things up
when needed.

The tongs was even used to make toast when placed
flat over the fire.

As bedtime approaches the blaze gives way to dark
red coals.

Reminding sleepy eyes that the day is over and it's
time for dreamland.

By morning the fading embers will have turned to
whitish ash.

Another roaring fire will replace the old one with
wise words from Da:

'Let ye get a good heat goin out in the mornin and it
will stay with ye'.

A reek of turf was a natural part of the landscape
outside most houses.

Turf fires are rare enough nowadays, and the bogs
are tourist attractions.

At least the memory of another era will live on when
the turf fire is well gone.

NAN'S BED

This is the bed where I lay
And slept all my care's away
Alone and in solitude
An odd prayer to St Jude

Sometimes I could not sleep
Then into the past I would peep
I thought of my family
All of them started from me

Da by now had passed on
The rest of them sing their song
There's Pa and Sean and Matt
I thought I'd leave it at that

Then Tommy Brendan and Stephen
At six the number was even
But so far no girl I had
I thought it a little sad

Then along came Joe
And I said: 'again here we go'
My patience finally repaid
When Maureen her entry made

Three more children there's been
Ger, Patricia, Eileen
Patricia is an angel in Heaven
A sacrifice freely given

So now my bed is made
And my prayers I've said
God has a place for me
To rest for eternity

ARE THE DAFFODILS UP

In my last book I wrote of my Father's death, so this chapter is of my Mother's.
It's a sad time but it happens to all, and it's just as natural as birth.
We called her 'Nan', and our yearly question on the phone was:
'Are the daffodils up yet Nan'?
'Oh, they are up and there's even buds on some of them', she might say.
You could hear the joy in her voice, because she loved the Spring.
Naturally enough she was born in the Spring, and died in the autumn.
She had a great sense of wonder, and she loved the flowers and the birds.
'Aren't they lovely', she'd say, staring at a bunch of primroses.
She had daily birds, and seasonal flowers.
The blackbird in the morning, the robin and thrush, and the afternoon lark.
The unique sound of the minnaun blended in with the balmy summer evenings.
Nan's flower season started with the daffodil, though the snowdrop had come and gone.
Buttercups, primroses, mayflowers, bluebells, daisies, and the last rose of summer.

She had wonderful sayings which always ended with: 'did you ever heard it said'.

'Where there's a will there's a way', did you ever heard it said.

When we couldn't wait for the summer holidays she'd say: 'Too soon they'll come and go'.

'There's so much good in the worst of us, and so much bad in the best of us,

That it ill behoves any of us, to speak about the rest of us', went another saying.

An unusual one of her's for the times she lived in was: 'Spend and God will send'.

'It's not the day of the wind the days of the scollop', and so her sayings went.

Nan could often be found 'out the back' feeding her hens of many colours.

She had a good sense of humour which kept her calm when the going got tough.

That's just some small memories of my Mother, but important ones.

She passed away on Sunday the 14th August 2005, at the age of 88.

The rain fell gently on her coffin as she was laid to rest in her native Guesdian.

Shortly after her death her friend, Rose Collins, had a beautiful dream.

This vivid dream saw them both walking through a field of flowers:

THE FIELD OF FLOWERS

Walking in the field of flowers
When this life on earth is through
Flowers that will never wither
In a land that's ever new.

All the colours of the rainbow
In this place of rosy hue
Aches and pains now disappearing
Light-foot in the morning dew

In the distance stands the Shepherd
Waving gently 'come to me'
'Let me wipe the tears of sorrow
Never more those tears shall be'.

All the suffering now has meaning
When we view it from this place
All the sadness all the crosses
T'was a time of gentle grace.

Grief and sadness left on earth
We will mourn for a while
Then we'll carry on our journey
With the memory of Nan's smile

MY OWN MEMORIES

TIME

And so time rolls by, and we wonder why?
Why we were chosen to live in this particular period
of history.
This day, this week, this month, this year, this
century, this millennium.
Whatever the reason this is our time, so we better
make the most of it.
We are often grappling with time, as it seems to go
too fast or too slow.
However the clock ticks on normally, and is not
concerned by human reactions.
Things take more time to do than we think, but we
have more time than we think.
Some people talk about buying time, or perhaps
borrowing time.
We'd like to bottle time and take it down when we
think we most need it.
Perhaps the clock is the closest we have come to
bottling time.
The old grandfather clock ticked us into time, as the
heart ticked us into life.
The clock ticked calmly away as the heart gave its
final tick at the end of life.
At this moment people are entering this organism
called time, while others are leaving.

The first atomic clock was built in the USA in the year 1948.
It loses a second every 30,000 years; ah well nothing's perfect.
No matter how much we fight or try to master time it will always win.
To live one day at a time is the great secret if we can manage it at all.
We often have one eye on yesterday and the other on tomorrow, crying on today.
It's good to untangle the past and have our dreams for the future, but live the day.
We can drown out God's Providence by preparing excessively for the future.
We often let a golden moment pass by thinking a better one is coming along.
There is a power in the present moment which could change everything.
Whether we say time is running out, or how will I pass the time, it's always now.
With a little planning we could easily make time our friend instead of our enemy.
Interestingly most of our generation have lived in two different millenniums.
A thousand years of time will pass before that happens again.
Anyway that's enough about time except to say: it's time to say goodbye. GOODBYE.

AUTUMENNIUM

Walking through the brown leaves in Clogher
Soothing rhythm between thought and sound
The golden foggy sun sinks beneath the skyline
Trees go to bed or death for the winter
Only to bud again in a new time

Sheep without a shepherd on the hillside
The last wildflower shaking in the wind
'Tis the end of the century, and even the
Millennium

Walking by the sea of Galilee setting men free
Never heard of Millennium even if he started it
Lived the past and the future in the present
Seeing with different eyes the old to new
The first shall be last and the last first

Watched the ripples grow from a pebble
Like the great tree from a mustard seed
2000 years on what is the worlds song

Walking through the brown leaves of Clogher
Pondering the future, meditating the past
Must bridge the two and live the present
One day at a time and drink new wine

The vanished sun leaves a red western sky
The millenniums autumn is sinking too
Sometimes the darkness must be entered
In the distance the cry of a new-born baby